W9-BST-443

Ella the Rose Fairy

To Lily Grace Evans,
who will always believe in fairies

Special thanks to Sue Mongredien

If you purchased this book without a cover, you should be aware that this book is stolen property. It was reported as "unsold and destroyed" to the publisher, and neither the author nor the publisher has received any payment for this "stripped book."

No part of this work may be reproduced, stored in a retrieval system, or transmitted in any form or by any means, electronic, mechanical, photocopying, recording, or otherwise, without written permission of the publisher. For information regarding permission, write to Rainbow Magic Limited c/o HIT Entertainment, 830 South Greenville Avenue, Allen, TX 75002-3320.

ISBN-10: 0-545-07096-1
ISBN-13: 978-0-545-07096-6

Copyright © 2007 by Rainbow Magic Limited.

All rights reserved. Published by Scholastic Inc., 557 Broadway, New York, NY 10012, by arrangement with Rainbow Magic Limited.

SCHOLASTIC, LITTLE APPLE, and associated logos are trademarks and/or registered trademarks of Scholastic Inc.
RAINBOW MAGIC is a trademark of Rainbow Magic Limited.
Reg. U.S. Patent & Trademark Office and other countries.

12 11 10 9 8 7 6 5 4 3 2 1 9 10 11 12 13/0

Printed in the U.S.A.

First Scholastic Printing, February 2009

Ella the Rose Fairy

by Daisy Meadows

SCHOLASTIC INC.
New York Toronto London Auckland Sydney
Mexico City New Delhi Hong Kong Buenos Aires

The Fairyland Palace
Blossom Hall
Fairy Garden
Leafley Village
Visitors' Center

Jack Frost's
Ice Castle
m Lake
Picnic Spot
Park
Petal Perfection
Flower Shop
Blossom Village
High St.
Rainbow Falls Gardens
aney Court Flower Show

I need the magic petals' powers,
To give my castle garden flowers.
I plan to use my magic well
To work against the fairies' spell.

From my wand ice magic flies,
Frosty bolts through fairy skies.
This is the crafty spell I weave
To bring the petals back to me.

Contents

Roses Need Rescuing!	1
Maze Magic	15
Pink Lightning	25
A Frosty Atmosphere	35
Frozen Flowers	45
A New Friend	55

Roses Need Rescuing!

"Here we are, the Chaney Court Flower Show," Mr. Walker said, looking at the steady stream of people heading toward the entrance. He smiled at his daughter, Rachel, and her best friend, Kirsty Tate. "What a flower-filled week we've had!"

"We love flowers!" Rachel said, giving Kirsty a secret smile.

"Especially since we met the Petal Fairies," Kirsty agreed in a whisper.

The girls linked arms as they followed their parents into the field where the flower show was taking place. The two families had been spending spring vacation together, and the girls had been helping the Petal Fairies find their missing magic petals. They had found six petals so far, but there was still one more to track down — the rose petal.

"What's in here?" Mr. Tate wondered aloud, as they approached a large tent.

"Ah, the rose tent," he said, reading the sign on the entrance.

Kirsty and Rachel exchanged excited glances. Maybe the missing rose petal would be inside!

A group of people were leaving the tent as the Tates and the Walkers approached.

"How disappointing," a man said gloomily. "I've never seen such unhealthy flowers!"

The Tates and the Walkers stepped inside the tent and Rachel saw that the man was right. All the roses were drooping, their petals faded and withered.

Rachel bit her lip. She and Kirsty knew exactly why the roses weren't doing well. The Petal Fairies' magic petals helped flowers grow in Fairyland and around the world. But cruel Jack Frost had sent his goblins to steal the petals. He wanted to use the petals' magic to make flowers bloom around his ice castle. When the Petal Fairies had tried to stop the goblins, the magic petals were caught in a whirl of spells and ended up in the human world! Now that the petals were missing, flowers everywhere were wilting and dying.

"Let's go and see some of the gardens instead," Mr. Walker suggested, looking sadly at the drooping roses.

Rachel turned to Kirsty as they left. "Most of the flowers should be beautiful because we've already found the six other petals and sent them back to Fairyland," she whispered.

Kirsty nodded. "But we have to rescue these roses! I bet all the dark pink flowers in the show are dying," she added.

The Petal Fairies had told the girls that each magic petal looked after its own type of flower, and other flowers of a particular color. The rose petal helped roses and all dark pink flowers grow.

"We've got to find the petal before the goblins do," Rachel whispered. "It's their last chance to take a petal back to Jack Frost. I'm sure they'll be trying extra hard to find this one!"

The girls knew that the goblins were trying to find the fairy petals for their boss. And to make things even harder for Kirsty and Rachel, Jack Frost had given his goblins a wand full of his icy magic to use against them.

As the two families wandered down the path, Kirsty could see that the display

gardens were lined up in one long row, each in a separate area.

"What a beautiful Japanese garden!" her mom exclaimed, stopping at the first garden. "Look at that bamboo."

"And isn't the fountain pretty?" Mrs. Walker added.

Rachel couldn't concentrate on the Japanese garden, though, because she'd just spotted the sign outside the next area. It read "Fairy Garden."

She nudged Kirsty. "Look!"

The fairy garden had an iron gate at its entrance and was filled with flowers in all colors of the rainbow. There was a winding path made of glittering stones, and a bench perfect for relaxing . . . and looking for fairies!

"Mom, can we go into the fairy garden?" Kirsty asked.

Mrs. Tate smiled. "Of course,"

she said. "Why don't we split up and meet you later? How about one hour from now in the refreshments tent?"

"Perfect!" Kirsty said, as her parents waved good-bye and walked on to look at the other gardens.

"Come on, Rachel! The Petal Fairies would love it here," Kirsty said, pushing open the gate and walking in.

"Definitely," Rachel agreed, following her friend. Then, suddenly, she stopped. "Kirsty, look!"

Kirsty followed Rachel's gaze to see a large, healthy-looking rose bush covered with dark pink flowers in the back corner of the garden. "The magic petal must be near that bush." Kirsty gasped. "Otherwise, the roses wouldn't look so beautiful!"

"Yes," Rachel said happily. "So — Uh-oh!" She broke off as she noticed that the rose bush was rustling. "It's moving!"

Kirsty's smile vanished. "What if the goblins are in there?"

Luckily, there was nobody else in the garden, so the girls were able to tiptoe down the path and over to the rustling roses. Cautiously, they peeked around the side of the bush.

Seven horrible goblins were pulling all the roses

off the bush! They were wearing little boys' clothes, clearly hoping to blend in with the other visitors at the show. The goblins were busy picking through the roses to find the magic petal.

"Ugh, pink!" the girls heard one goblin complain. "Such an ugly color!"

"Green is much better," another agreed.

Kirsty looked at Rachel with wide eyes, wondering how they were going to find the petal before the goblins did.

Just then, a silvery voice echoed through the air behind them. "Hello, girls! I love your pink outfits."

Kirsty and Rachel spun around to see a smiling fairy fluttering in the air!

"Ella!" Kirsty cried, stepping away from the rose bush so that she could speak to the fairy without being overheard.

"We're so glad to see you!" Rachel added.

Ella the Rose Fairy had long, dark, wavy hair and wore a pink dress with a sash around the middle.

As she opened her mouth to speak to the girls, an excited cry came from behind the rose bush.

Kirsty, Rachel, and Ella all peeked through the leaves. To their dismay, they saw that one of the goblins was holding out his hands . . . and the magic rose petal was lying in them! Rachel thought quickly. "Ella, could you use your fairy magic to make the petal float out of his hands — and over here, to us?" she suggested.

"Yes!" Ella replied eagerly, pointing her wand at the bush.

A stream of sparkles swirled from the tip of her wand and over the thorny branches.

The girls held their breath as they watched the sparkles surround the magic petal, lift it into the air, and carry it back over the bush. The plan was working!

But then a green hand appeared and snatched the petal back.

"Oh, no you don't. You're staying with us!" the girls heard a goblin say.

"What's going on?" another asked. Then three goblin faces appeared around the side of the bush.

"We should have guessed," sneered one. "It's those silly girls with a silly fairy."

"Searching for the petal, are you?" another gloated. "Too bad!"

"May I please have it?" Ella asked sweetly. "It *is* mine, you know!"

"Not anymore, it isn't!" The goblin holding the petal laughed. "It's ours. And we're bringing it to Jack Frost. He'll be very happy with us!"

Just then, one of the goblins burst out laughing, pointing at the girls and Ella. "Look at them, all wearing yucky pink!" he cackled.

"Pink stinks!" another yelled. "We're out of here!"

And with that, the goblins rushed out of the back of the fairy garden, taking the rose petal with them.

"Follow them!" Kirsty cried.

Ella swooped down to hide under Rachel's hair as the girls raced after the goblins. The goblins ran past an English cottage garden, then a rock garden, before turning into a maze of hedges.

Kirsty had just enough time to glimpse the sign as she ran by. It read, *Chaney Court Hedge Maze. Can you find the statue in the middle?*

The goblins scattered, each charging down different paths.

"Which one has the petal?" Rachel cried, not sure which goblin to chase.

"I'll turn you both into fairies," Ella decided. "Then we can fly and hopefully spot the petal from above!"

In a shower of pink sparkles, Kirsty and Rachel found themselves shrinking to fairy-size.

Gorgeous, glittery wings appeared on their backs, and they immediately zoomed up above the maze. "I can see three goblins," Kirsty said, pointing them out. "Oh, and there's another. . . ." "There's one in the middle, by the statue," Rachel added. "And look at what he's holding!" "My petal!" Ella cried joyfully.

The three friends zipped toward the statue. "Ella, if you turn us back to our normal size, Rachel and I can try to get your petal back from him," Kirsty suggested.

Ella lifted her wand, but Rachel stopped her.

"Hold on," she said, pointing down at the maze. "The other goblins are almost at the center, too. I don't think we'll be able to get the petal away from all of them."

Ella nodded. "Let me make the maze a little bit more difficult for them," she said with a sly grin.

She flitted over and sprinkled some fairy dust along the path that led to the center of the maze. Instantly, a new section of hedge started to grow, blocking the entrance to the clearing where the statue stood.

The goblin who was already standing by the statue stared at the new hedge. "Hey! I'm trapped!" he yelled.

"And his friends won't be able to come to his rescue!" Kirsty realized with a giggle. "Super smart, Ella!"

Rachel grinned. "Now let's get that petal!" she cried.

Rachel and Kirsty swooped down to the center of the maze. Once they landed, Ella turned them back into girls with another wave of her wand.

The goblin was surprised to see them appear in front of him. "Help! Those girls have found me!" he shouted in alarm.

Kirsty grinned. "You can shout as much as you want, but they won't be able to help you."

Rachel held out her hand. "You might as well give us the petal now," she told him, "because you're trapped in here with us!"

The goblin hid the petal behind his back. "I'm not giving it to you," he said stubbornly.

"Hang on! We're coming!" another goblin's voice called from somewhere over the hedge.

"It's no use," the goblin with the petal shouted back. "I'm stuck in here with their pesky fairy magic!"

"Well, those fairies should know by now that we have our own magic!" came another shout. The girls jumped and looked around, because the voice sounded very close behind them.

There was a rustling noise, and Rachel and Kirsty turned to see a wand poking through the hedge — a wand held by a goblin's green hand!

Before the girls could do or say anything, one of the goblins started chanting a spell.

"This will stop those girls, I think. Lightning bolts, zap all things pink!" he cried from the other side of the hedge.

Kirsty looked down at her top in horror. She was wearing pink — and so were Rachel and Ella. They were all about to get blasted by the goblins' icy magic! "Hide!" yelled Kirsty, ducking behind the statue. The next instant, lightning bolts fizzed through the hedge right at her.

CRASH! One bolt hit the statue — and to the girls' surprise, it turned the statue bright pink!

CRASH! Another bolt struck the goblin with the petal.

Rachel and Kirsty stared at him in shock. He had turned pink, right before their eyes!

Ella gave a tinkling laugh. "It's because of the way the goblin said the spell," she explained. "When he said 'Lightning bolts, zap all things pink', he wanted for lightning to strike everything that's pink—but instead, it's *turning* things pink!"

The goblin with the petal didn't seem to notice his color change. "It didn't work!" he shouted through the hedge. "The lightning missed that pesky pink fairy and her friends!"

Three goblins peered through the hedge — and immediately burst into laughter. "Hey, pink looks good on you!" one of them teased.

"What?" demanded the goblin with

the petal. He looked down at himself and gasped. "I'm pink!" he wailed.

"It's definitely your color." Rachel giggled.

"Very flattering," Ella agreed, sputtering with laughter.

"It's not funny!" the pink goblin snapped, stomping his foot. "Turn me green again right now!"

Once the goblins on the other side of the hedge had managed to stop laughing, the wand poked through the branches again. The girls heard another goblin clear his throat, to cast a second spell.

"Oh, no you don't!" Kirsty cried, darting forward and snatching the wand right out of his hand.

"Hey!" came a surprised shout. "Give that back!"

"No way," Kirsty replied happily. But she then gulped in alarm, because the magic hedge plants that Ella had conjured up suddenly vanished in a burst of pink sparkles. And, all at once, the other goblins charged into the middle of the maze!

A Frosty Atmosphere

Ella quickly turned the girls back into fairies, so they could zoom up into the air and escape the goblins. The goblins' wand in Kirsty's hand became fairy-sized, too.

"Hey — give our wand back!" one of the goblins shouted.

"Jack Frost will be mad if we come back without it," another said, worried. He jumped up, trying to catch the girls.

"Sorry, guys!" Rachel grinned. "But —" She broke off as she spotted a girl in a lilac T-shirt walking close to the center of the maze. "Oh no!" Rachel gulped. "Look!" "We can't let her see the goblins!" Ella cried.

Kirsty's mind raced, until she remembered she had a magic wand in her hand. She quickly pointed it down at the goblins and tried to think up a spell. "Whisk this magic far away, back to Jack Frost's hideaway!" she declared.

A magical wind began to blow around the goblins, sweeping them up into the air. But then Kirsty felt a cold wind tugging at her, too.

"Oh no!" Ella exclaimed. "We're part of the magic, too. We're caught up in the spell!"

Kirsty gulped as the wind grew even stronger. "You mean . . ." she began.

Ella nodded. "We're on our way to Jack Frost!"

Everything blurred before the girls' eyes as they were whisked up in the magical whirlwind with the goblins.

When the whirl of magic finally died away, the girls and Ella saw that they were hovering in midair, a short distance from Jack Frost's ice castle. Below them, the goblins were lying in the snow, a heap of tangled arms and legs.

Jack Frost turned in surprise, from where he'd been feeding his snow geese at the pond.

"Oh, it's you!" he snapped at the goblins. "What do you have for me?" Kirsty, Rachel, and Ella quickly fluttered behind a nearby tree, hoping Jack Frost wouldn't notice them. Luckily, his eye was drawn straight to the goblin at the bottom of the heap, who was still bright pink. "What on Earth . . .?" Jack Frost sputtered. "What have you been doing?"

"It wasn't my fault!" the pink goblin moaned. "Besides, look what I brought for you!" he added proudly, wiggling his hand out from under the other goblins. He was still clutching the rose petal between his fingers.

"At last! A magic petal of my own!" Jack Frost cried triumphantly. "Now I will have all the flowers I want growing around my castle!"

Poor Ella could hardly watch. "If Jack Frost gets his hands on my petal, I might never see it again," she whispered miserably.

"What if Kirsty and I distract him?" Rachel suggested. "Then you can fly over and grab the petal while he's not looking!"

"OK!" Ella said, her face brightening. "Let's try it."

As Ella headed toward the petal, the girls flew out into the open, behind Jack Frost.

Kirsty saw that Jack Frost was just reaching out to grab the petal.

"Hey, Jack Frost!" she called quickly. "Aren't you wondering where your wand is?"

Jack Frost turned in surprise, and glared when he saw Kirsty and Rachel.

"We've got it!" Rachel added.

"And we're going to cast a spell on you!" Kirsty cried.

"How did you get my wand?" Jack Frost bellowed furiously.

He immediately marched away from

the goblins, toward the girls. "I'll take that, thank you," he snapped. He stared hard at the wand, then lifted his hand and muttered a magic word. Instantly, the wand flew from Kirsty's grasp back to its master.

With a horrible grin, Jack Frost pointed the wand at the girls. "Maybe this will teach you to stop causing trouble!" he told them. And then, as he whispered a spell, a freezing lightning bolt came shooting out of the wand — straight toward Rachel and Kirsty.

Frozen Flowers

"Hide!" shouted Rachel. Quickly, she and Kirsty hid behind the tree trunk. Neither of them could see Ella now, but they both really hoped she'd been able to grab her petal.

Kirsty peeked around the tree to look for Ella, and then pulled back in alarm as two more lightning bolts flashed past. She and Rachel clung to each other.

"What are we going to do?" Kirsty asked as lightning bolts whistled past the tree, barely missing the girls. "I don't know," Rachel replied. "Sooner or later, one of these is going to hit us!"

But as the girls looked at each other in panic, Kirsty saw a stream of pink fairy dust sparkling in the sky above them. As she watched, the fairy dust began to turn into brightly colored flowers that rained down to the ground between the girls and Jack Frost. More and more of them appeared in the sky and floated down, creating a curtain of falling flowers. And when Jack Frost's lightning bolts hit the bright blooms, they bounced right off.

"The flowers are acting like a shield," Kirsty realized.

"It must be petal magic!" Rachel cried in delight.

"And, look, there are the Petal Fairies!" Kirsty exclaimed, pointing to where Ella was flitting in the air, along with the other Petal Fairies: Tia, Pippa, Louise, Charlotte, Olivia, and Danielle. They were all smiling and waving at Kirsty and Rachel.

"Ella must have rescued her petal when we distracted Jack Frost." Rachel laughed. "And now all of the Petal Fairies have come to rescue us!"

Kirsty nodded happily. "Look!" she said, pointing to the curtain of flowers. "When the icy lightning bolts hit the magic wall, they freeze the falling flowers. Aren't they pretty?"

Rachel grinned. "Yes. And, look — Jack Frost obviously thinks so, too!" She pointed to Jack Frost, who was no longer hurling lightning bolts at the girls. Instead, he was bending down and scooping up armfuls of the frozen flowers.

"Hey, you guys!" he shouted to his goblins. "Come and help me gather all of these. They're perfect for decorating my castle gardens!"

The goblins, who'd untangled themselves by now, ran over to help. "Look at these frozen sunflowers!" one of them exclaimed. "They'll look good over here," he added, planting them in the ground. Being frozen, they stood up straight and sparkled brilliantly with frost.

"These tulips are nice," another goblin sighed. "I think I'll take a bunch home to my mom."

Ella and the other Petal Fairies flew down to join the girls.

"Thank you for saving us from Jack Frost," Kirsty said.

Ella laughed. "We're the ones who should be thanking you," she told the girls. "You did a great job — again!"

Tia smiled. "Let's leave Jack Frost to his frozen flowers," she suggested, taking Kirsty by the hand.

Louise came over and took Rachel's hand. "Yes, let's go," she said.

"Where to?" Kirsty asked, feeling excited.

Olivia smiled. "To the Fairyland palace, of course!" she said. "King Oberon and Queen Titania are waiting to see you!"

A New Friend

The seven Petal Fairies led Kirsty and Rachel away from Jack Frost's castle to the beautiful gardens outside the Fairyland palace. There, the girls saw the fairy king and queen waiting for them. They were standing next to a pool that glittered in the sunlight.

"Good job!" Queen Titania said

warmly as the girls landed. "We watched everything right here, in the seeing pool. Rachel and Kirsty, you have done a fantastic job helping the fairies get all seven of their magic petals back."

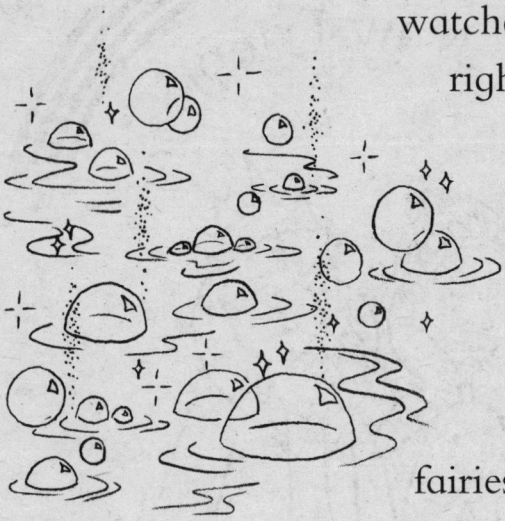

"Yes, we couldn't have done it without them," Charlotte the Sunflower Fairy said, beaming.

"And now that Jack Frost has his everlasting ice flowers, he won't bother our Petal Fairies again," the king added. He shook his head, looking frustrated. "If he had just come and asked us for help in the first place, none of this would have happened. He didn't need to steal the petals."

"Yes!" Queen Titania said. "We certainly understand that flowers are meant to be shared. I'm glad Jack Frost is happy with his palace garden now."

Then Ella waved her wand over Kirsty and Rachel and, to their surprise, garlands of rainbow-colored flowers appeared around their necks.

"Thank you!" Rachel exclaimed. "They're beautiful!"

"Of course," Ella replied. "They're just a little something to remember the Petal Fairies by."

The queen lifted her wand. "I'm afraid it's time for you to return to the human world now," she said.

"Oh, yes, we're supposed to be meeting our parents soon," Kirsty agreed.

"Good-bye, girls," Ella said, giving Rachel and Kirsty a last hug. "And thanks again!"

"Good-bye," the two girls chorused.

The queen waved her wand over them,

and they were whisked away from Fairyland in a blur of color. Seconds later, they found themselves back in the maze, and at their normal size.

"It's strange being here without Ella or the goblins," Kirsty said, looking around.

Rachel nodded. "It's so much more quiet!" She laughed.

"And look," Kirsty said, "our flower garlands have turned into necklaces. Aren't they pretty?"

Rachel saw that Kirsty was right — they were both wearing necklaces made of glittering, flower-shaped beads. There were seven different beads that matched the colors of the magic petals. The necklaces were almost as beautiful as the real flowers!

Just then, a girl with a lilac T-shirt walked into the center of the maze.

Of course! Kirsty thought. *It's the girl who was about to reach the middle when we were whisked away to Fairyland.*

"Hi," said the girl. "My name's Arabella Diers. This maze is hard, isn't it? It's taken me forever to get here!"

"I'm Rachel," Rachel replied. She didn't know what to say about the maze. After all, she and Kirsty had flown to the middle. They hadn't actually had to find their way through the maze at all. Suddenly, she realized that they didn't have a clue how to get out!

"It is hard," Kirsty was saying. "In fact, we can't remember the way out. Can you?"

Arabella nodded. "I think so," she said. "Follow me!" As she turned to lead the way out, she caught sight of the girls' necklaces. "Ooh! They're pretty," she commented.

It didn't take the three girls long to find the start of the maze.

"Here we are!" Arabella said proudly as they reached the exit.

"Thank you," Kirsty said. Impulsively, she pulled off her fairy necklace and handed it to Arabella. "Here — have this," she said. "To say thanks for helping us." Arabella's face lit up.

"Oh, thank you!" she breathed, looking starry-eyed with delight. Rachel and Kirsty grinned. "That was nice of you," Rachel said, taking her own necklace off as Arabella walked away. "If you like, we could try and make my necklace into anklets. Then we can each have one."

Suddenly, she gasped as the necklace started to shimmer with a sparkly pink light. As the girls watched, the necklace split apart and transformed itself into two pretty anklets.

Kirsty stared at Rachel, her mouth wide open. "How did you do that?" she gasped.

Rachel was just as surprised as Kirsty. "I didn't do anything! The fairies must have been watching over us," she said with a smile. "Thank you, Petal Fairies!" She handed an anklet to Kirsty, and both girls fastened them around their ankles.

"We'd better go and meet our parents," Rachel said. "Come on!"

The girls rushed over to the refreshments tent, just in time to see their parents sitting down by a beautiful, flowering rose bush. "Aren't these fantastic?" Mrs. Walker said to Rachel and Kirsty, sniffing one of the blooms.

"Yes, and you wouldn't believe it, but when we passed the rose tent a minute ago, all the roses were looking much better!" Mr. Tate put in.

The girls exchanged happy glances.

Now that the rose petal was back in Fairyland, it was working its special magic all over the world again. Roses and dark pink flowers everywhere would be growing beautifully!

Mr. Walker smiled at the girls. "Did you have fun?" he asked.

"Yes, thanks," Rachel told him. "The maze was really good."

"Yes, it was a lot of fun!" Kirsty added. The two girls grinned at one another. They both loved their fairy adventures. Being friends with the fairies made *everything* fun!

Rachel and Kirsty helped all seven Petal Fairies, but now there's more trouble in Fairyland. The Dance Fairies need their help!

Join the adventure in this special sneak peek of

Bethany the Ballet Fairy!

Fairies in a Whirl

"I'm really excited about this!" exclaimed Rachel Walker, smiling at her best friend, Kirsty Tate. "I *love* ballet."

"Me, too," Kirsty agreed, raising her voice above the noise of the train as it rattled over the bumpy tracks. "I've never seen *Swan Lake* before."

"I've heard that this is a great

production," Kirsty's mom said. "The scenery is supposed to be beautiful."

"Well, let's hope it keeps Dad awake!" Kirsty laughed, glancing at her dad. He was fast asleep in the corner seat of the train. "I'm so glad you could come, Rachel. Wasn't it lucky that your school got out for vacation the day before ours did? You wouldn't have been here in time to come with us, otherwise."

Rachel nodded. Because their families lived far apart, she was staying with Kirsty for the whole week of the school vacation.

"We'll be in the city soon," said Mrs. Tate, as the train pulled into a station. "This is the last stop before we get there."

Kirsty stared out the window as the train slowed. Suddenly, her attention was caught by a flash of icy blue streaking past. Curious, Kirsty leaned forward for a closer look.

To her amazement, she saw seven little fairies tumbling through the air on a tiny icy whirlwind! As Kirsty watched, the fairies landed safely in one of the baskets of flowers suspended from the station roof.

Kirsty and Rachel knew a lot about fairies because the two girls shared an amazing secret. They were best friends with the fairies! They often helped them to defeat Jack Frost and his nasty goblins, who were always causing trouble. Now it looked like their fairy friends might need the girls' help again!

There's magic in every boo

The Rainbow Fairies
Books #1–7

The Weather Fairies
Books #1–7

The Jewel Fair
Books #1–7

The Pet Fairies
Books #1–7

The Fun Day Fairies
Books #1–7

SCHOLASTIC and associated logos are trademarks and/or registered trademarks of Scholastic Inc.
©2008 Rainbow Magic Limited. Rainbow Magic is a trademark of Rainbow Magic Limited. Reg. U.S. Pat. & TM off. and other countries.
HIT and the HIT logo are trademarks of HIT Entertainment Limited.

SCHOLASTIC

www.scholastic.com

www.rainbowmagiconline.com